# FINDING FOXES

### ALLISON BLYLER

*Illustrated by*

### ROBERT J. BLAKE

PHILOMEL BOOKS • NEW YORK

For my grandmother, Marcia Lillard,
who knew how foxes sound,
and my mother, who knows how children sound
—A. L. B.

To my son, Christian
—R. J. B.

The leaves
on the breath
of the wind,
the fox in a
circle of sunlight.

The day was
gilt-edged
and so was
the fox.

The sound of a bird,
high and fine,
in the fox's ears.

The wind is
in waiting,
the tongue
on the lips
of the fox.

Dim, olive light
in the glen,
the fox
is hunting.

Six last leaves
fall, where
the fox once was.

The fox is
cruelly red,
in a knife of sun.

The fox
knows
what is real,
and what is
imagined.

I will always know
what is real,
but I can
weave an
imagination
of foxes.

Short, shiny barks,
of moonlight,
and foxes.

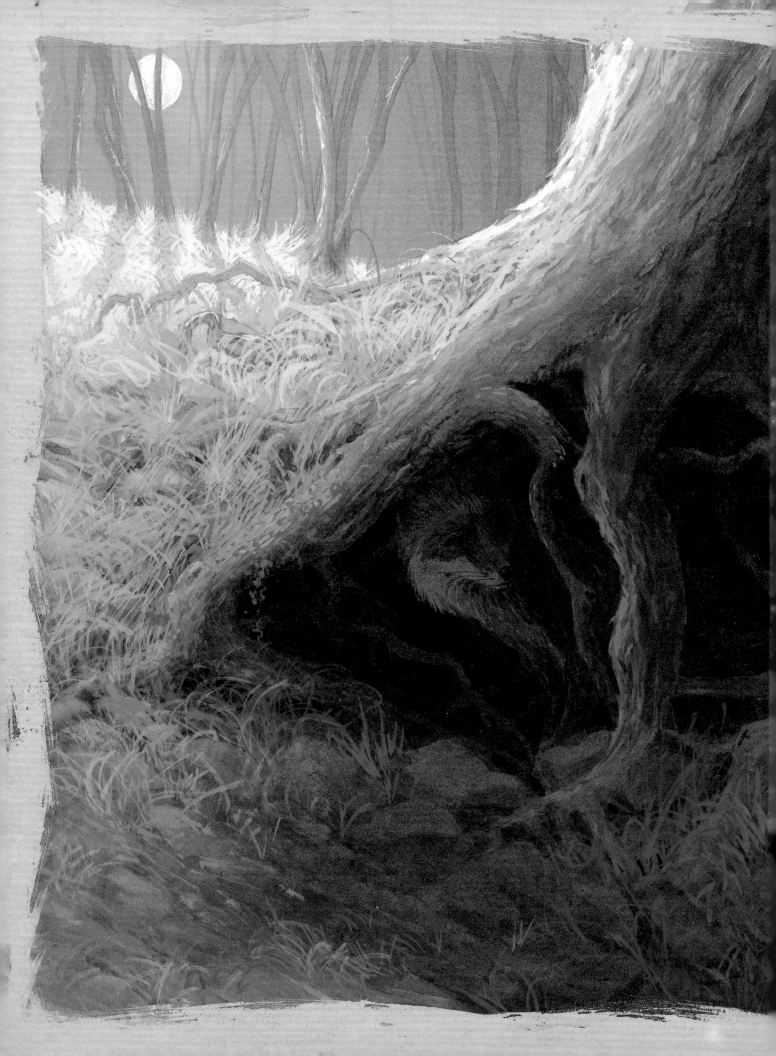

The shadows of
the trees
are foxes.

On the purpled hill,
the green fox
is alone,
I cannot share
his darkness.

If I imitate
the fox,
I cannot
change him.

I do not know
the ways of
the fox.
I ask
the river.

Text copyright © 1991 by Allison Blyler.

Illustrations copyright © 1991 by Robert J. Blake.

All rights reserved. This book, or parts thereof, may not be

reproduced in any form without permission in writing from the publisher.

Published by Philomel Books, a division of The Putnam & Grosset Book Group,

200 Madison Avenue, New York, NY 10016. Published simultaneously in Canada.

Printed in Hong Kong by South China Printing Co. (1988) Ltd.

Book design by Nanette Stevenson. Lettering by David Gatti.

The text is set in Garamond #3.

Library of Congress Cataloging-in-Publication Data

Blyler, Allison.

Finding foxes / by Allison Blyler ; illustrated by Robert Blake. p. cm.

Summary: The reader is invited to find hidden foxes in sunlight,

under waiting wind, and on a purpled hill. ISBN 0-399-22264-2

[1. Foxes—Fiction. 2. Picture puzzles.] I. Blake, Robert J.,

ill. II. Title. PZ7, B6277Fi 1991 [E]—dc20 90-35399 CIP AC

First impression